# The Spider Makes a Web

By JOAN M. LEXAU

Pictures by
ARABELLE WHEATLEY

HASTINGS HOUSE, PUBLISHERS, Inc.
New York 10016

The author and artist wish to thank Dr. Norman I. Platnick, Associate Curator, Arachnida, at the American Museum of Natural History, for providing invaluable assistance in the preparation of this book, and for the generous loan of one *Chalybion Ceruleum.*

Text copyright © 1979 by Joan M. Lexau. Illustrations copyright © 1979 by Arabelle Wheatley. This edition is published by Hastings House by arrangement with Scholastic Book Services, a division of Scholastic Magazines, Inc. All rights reserved. No part of this publication may be reproduced, stored in a retrieval system, or transmitted, in any form or by any means, electronic, mechanical, photocopying, recording or otherwise, without the prior permission of the copyright owner or the publishers.

Library of Congress Catalog Number: 78-75103

ISBN 0-8038-6766-2

Published simultaneously in Canada by Saunders of Toronto, Ltd., Don Mills, Ontario

*Printed in the United States of America*

*To Stephen Michael Klein*

It is spring.
The day is warm and dry.
It is a good day
for new little spiders
to find homes of their own.

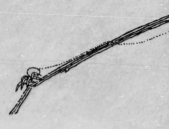

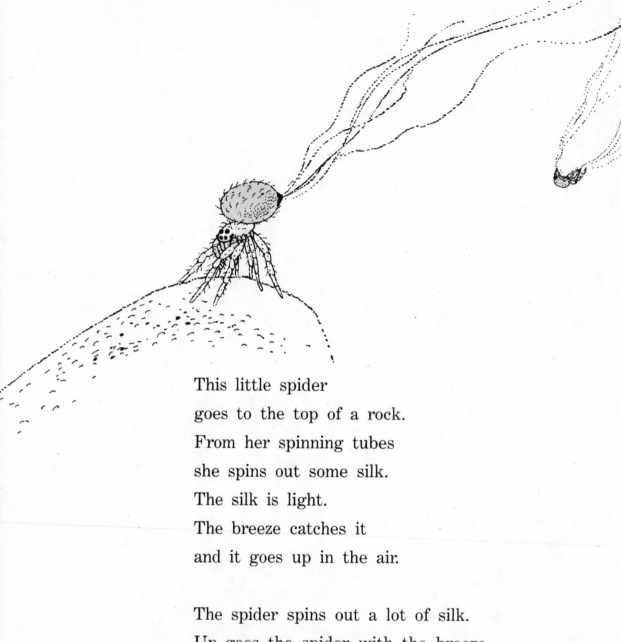

This little spider
goes to the top of a rock.
From her spinning tubes
she spins out some silk.
The silk is light.
The breeze catches it
and it goes up in the air.

The spider spins out a lot of silk.
Up goes the spider with the breeze
on her silk balloon.
Up in the air she goes,
way up in the sky.

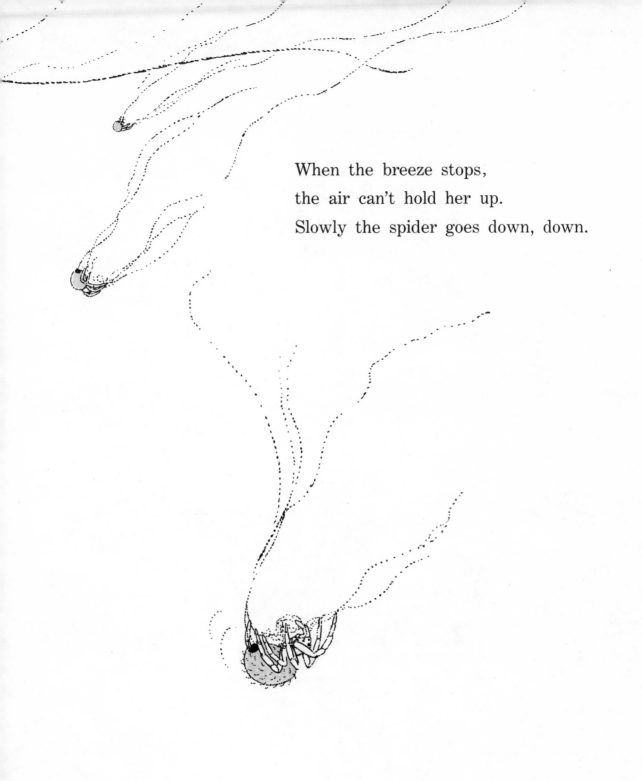

When the breeze stops,
the air can't hold her up.
Slowly the spider goes down, down.

She lands on the grass
near a blackberry bush.
This is a good spot
for her web.

The spider lets out some silk.
It goes up in the air.
She holds the other end
of the silk with the claws
on her feet.
The silk hits a branch
of the bush and sticks to it.
She sticks her end of the silk
to the grass.

11

Up the silk she runs to the branch.
Out goes more silk
to another branch.
Down to the ground the spider goes
letting out more silk.
This line she sticks
to the grass, too.
And now, with a new line of silk,
she runs to where she began her web.
The web has four sides now.

The spider makes a lot of straight lines
between the sides and the center of the web.
Then she runs around to make circle lines.
The circle lines will hold
the straight lines in place.

The spider goes to the outside of the web.
She begins to spin out sticky silk.
Around and around she goes,
making sticky lines,
until she gets back to the center of the web.
The lines will stay sticky for some time.
They will catch food for the spider.

Now she sticks silk
to the middle of the web.
She takes this silk line
along the branch
to a hiding place on the bush.
Here she makes a little tent
out of the leaves
and lines it with silk.
This is her place
to eat and sleep
away from the rain and wind.
She sticks the end of the line here.

Even in her sleep,
her claws hold onto the line.
The web moves a little.
The line pulls.
The spider feels the pull.
She runs on the line to the web
as fast as her eight legs can go.
She goes around and around
the thing that is stuck in the web.
She looks at it with her eight eyes.
Her eight eyes can't see much.
But she can tell if a thing
is big or little.
She can tell if something moves.

This thing is little.
She feels it
with her two feeler legs.
Her feelers are better
than her eyes.
It is a fly in her web.

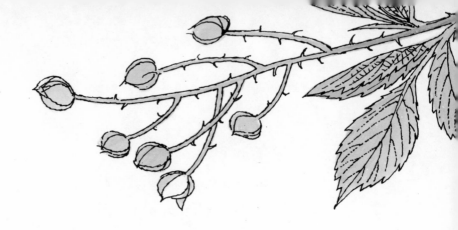

The spider sticks her fangs
into the fly.
The fly stops moving.
The spider pulls the fly
to her place in the bush.
Here the spider sucks the blood.
She pushes the dead fly
from the branch.
The spider rests.

All at once the line pulls hard.
Something big is shaking the web.
Down to the thing
the spider goes, but not too near.
At last she does go near.
But she is ready to run.
She feels a grasshopper.

The grasshopper is trying hard
to get away.
The spider turns her back.
She lets out some silk.
With her legs she wraps the grasshopper
around and around.

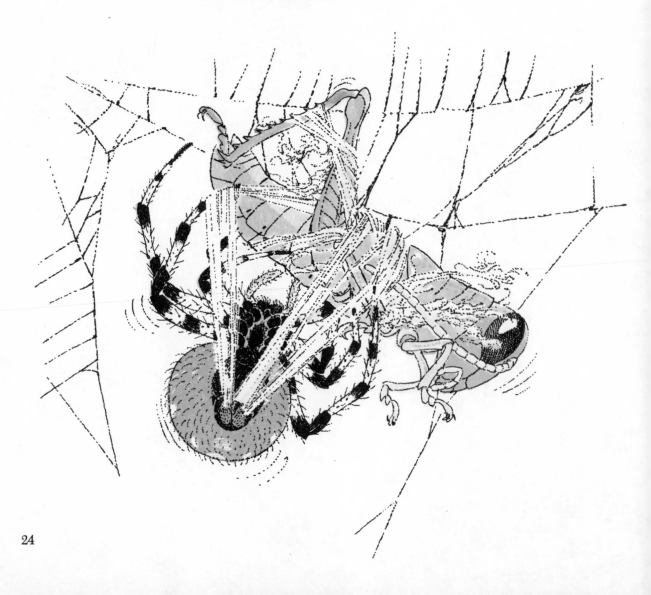

She covers it with silk.
Soon it looks like a mummy.
Now she can pull it
to her eating place.

A grasshopper is a lot of food for the spider.
But her stomach makes room for it.

The grasshopper has made holes
in the spider's web.
Now the spider takes down all
but the strong sides
and makes a new web inside.
She makes a new web
almost every day.

In the mornings
she has a drink of dew.
On her web or her branch,
she waits for more food.
The days go by.

One morning she goes out
on her web for a drink of dew.
Look out! Here comes a wasp.
The wasp wants food
for her children.
After the spider she goes.
The spider drops down
from the web.
She runs under a bush.

The wasp gets stuck in the web.
She pulls and tears at it
until she is free.
The wasp flies away.
But the web is broken.
The spider must make a new web.

As the spider grows bigger
she has to get out of her old skin.
She does this many times
before she is fully grown.
For a few days she does not eat.
One day she hangs upside down.
She wiggles and jerks.
Her skin cracks.
It starts to come off.
The skin on her legs
is hard to get off.
She wiggles and jerks and kicks
over and over and over.
At last the top skin is off.
She has a new skin.
The spider makes bigger webs now.
More days go by.

One day another spider comes
looking for a mate.
He drums on her web.
This is a sign.
It tells the spider
not to eat him.
Even so, she may eat him.

He doesn't stay long.
She is alone again.

It is fall now.
The spider is getting old.
It is time to lay her eggs.
First she must make
a basket of silk.
The eggs are laid in the basket.
The spider wraps the eggs
around and around, many times.

35

At last the eggs are as safe
as she can make them.
The spider goes away.
She is old.
In a few days she dies.

The baby spiders
come out of their eggs.
But they stay in the silk basket
until winter is over.
There is food for them
in the eggs.

When it is spring
the spiders make a hole
in the basket.
One by one they come out
and wait for a warm dry day.

Then the new little spiders
take to the air
to find homes of their own.

There are many kinds of spiders
that live in gardens and fields.
This book is about one such spider,
the Shamrock spider.
Scientists also call it
Araneus trifolium (**ar-e-nius tri-fol-ium**).